Sofia the First

A Royal Pet Problem

Adapted by Andrea Posner-Sanchez
from the script "Scrambled Pets" by Erica Rothschild
Illustrated by the Disney Storybook Art Team

Bath • New York • Cologne • Melbourne • Delhi
Hong Kong • Shenzhen • Singapore

Sofia, James, Amber and their friend Vivian are in the castle playground with their pets. Freedo, the baboon, is happily chasing a ball. Praline, the peacock, is trying to keep his feathers neat. Clover is eating, as usual! And an excited Crackle breathes fire.

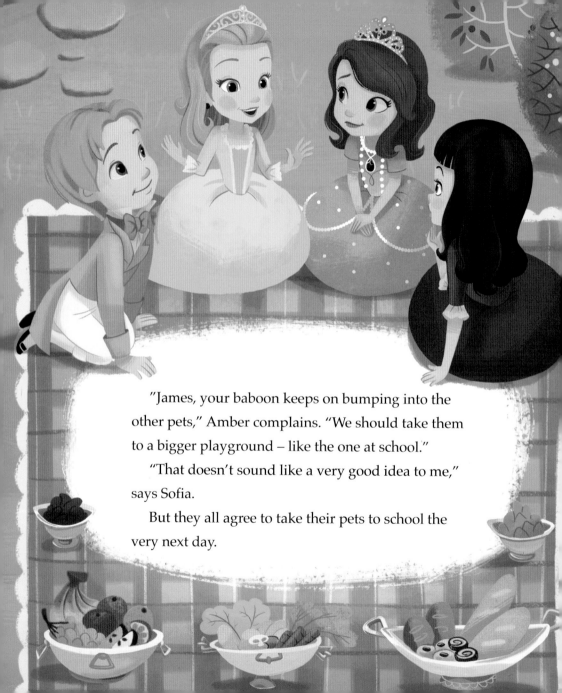

"James, your baboon keeps on bumping into the other pets," Amber complains. "We should take them to a bigger playground – like the one at school."

"That doesn't sound like a very good idea to me," says Sofia.

But they all agree to take their pets to school the very next day.

The following morning, Sofia, Amber, James and Vivian arrive at school with bigger bags than usual. But they won't have time to go to the playground until after sorcery class.

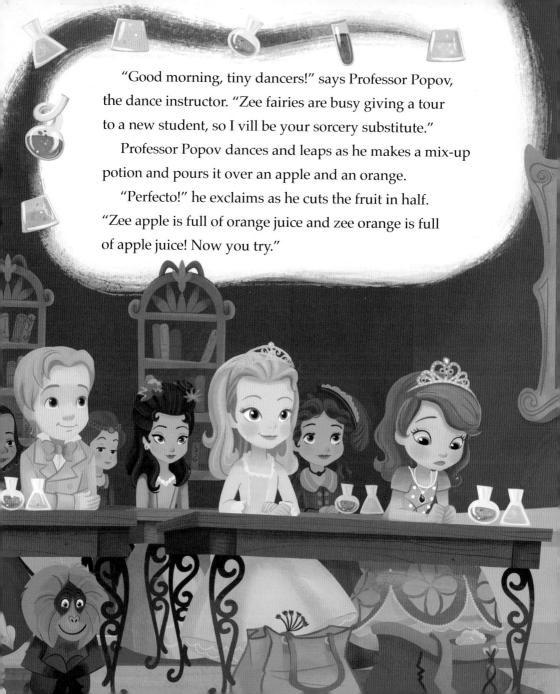

"Good morning, tiny dancers!" says Professor Popov, the dance instructor. "Zee fairies are busy giving a tour to a new student, so I vill be your sorcery substitute."

Professor Popov dances and leaps as he makes a mix-up potion and pours it over an apple and an orange.

"Perfecto!" he exclaims as he cuts the fruit in half. "Zee apple is full of orange juice and zee orange is full of apple juice! Now you try."

The professor hands out fruit to all of the students. Praline and Clover lick their lips and poke their heads out of their bags.

"You can eat later," Sofia whispers to them nervously.

When the professor twirls out of the classroom, Clover and Praline can no longer resist. They rush for an apple. Crackle tries to stop them and gets dragged along. Freedo leaps on to the pile of pets, bumping into a bottle of the mix-up potion along the way. The potion flies through the air – and spills on all four pets!

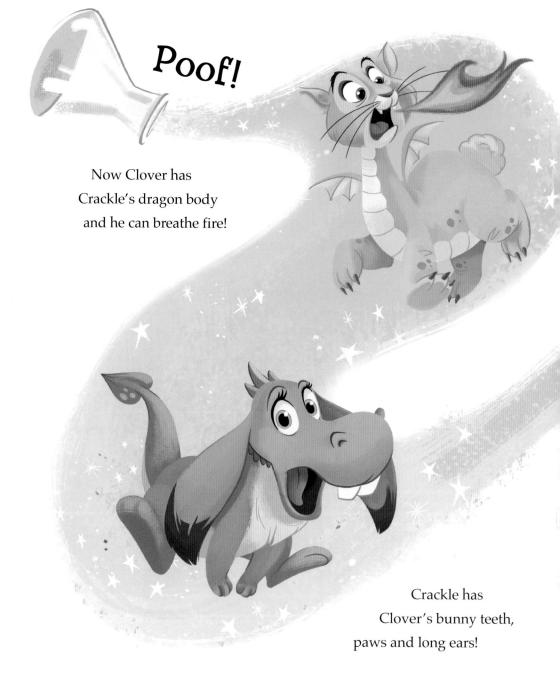

Poof!

Now Clover has
Crackle's dragon body
and he can breathe fire!

Crackle has
Clover's bunny teeth,
paws and long ears!

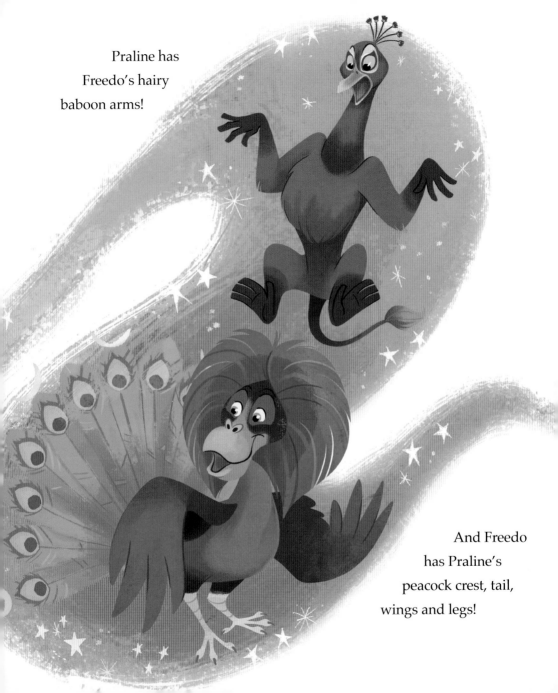

Praline has
Freedo's hairy
baboon arms!

And Freedo
has Praline's
peacock crest, tail,
wings and legs!

The students are stunned.

"Oh, this is bad!" cries Vivian. "This is really bad."

Just then, Freedo spots a ball and runs out of the door.

Praline chases him, yelling, "Come back here with my tail!"

"We have to get them back before the teachers see them!" James shouts.

Amber, James and Vivian head to the door.

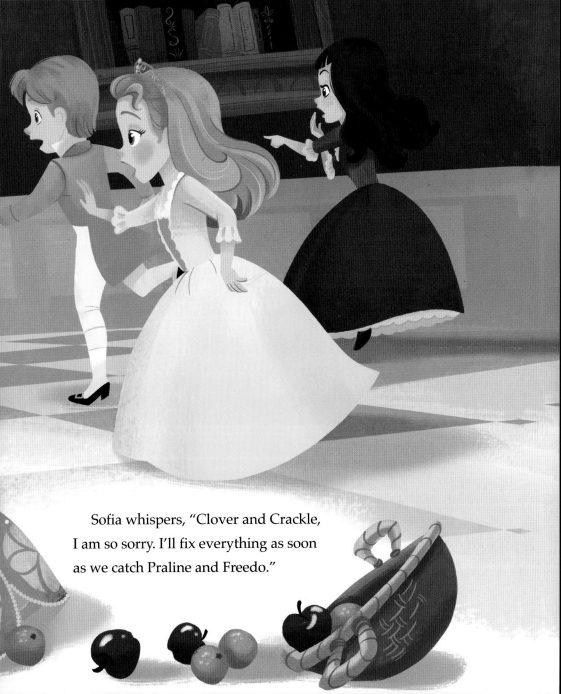

Sofia whispers, "Clover and Crackle,
I am so sorry. I'll fix everything as soon
as we catch Praline and Freedo."

Clover and Crackle are not happy.

"My nose burns and I'm covered in scales," Clover complains.

"Well, I'm covered in fur, and these ears keep hitting me in the face!" Crackle says.

They can't wait to get back to being themselves, so they decide to look for Freedo and Praline, too. But Clover isn't used to flying and Crackle isn't used to hopping!

From up in the air, Clover sees Praline and Freedo. "They're in the playground!" he reports. In all the excitement, a flame shoots out of Clover's mouth.

"See!" says Crackle. "That's what happens when I get excited."

"I'm beginning to understand that," Clover says, nervously holding on to the school roof.

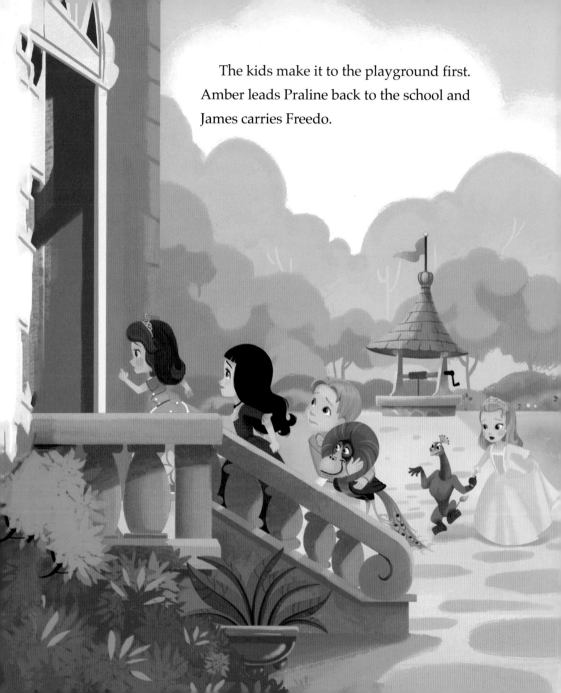

The kids make it to the playground first.
Amber leads Praline back to the school and
James carries Freedo.

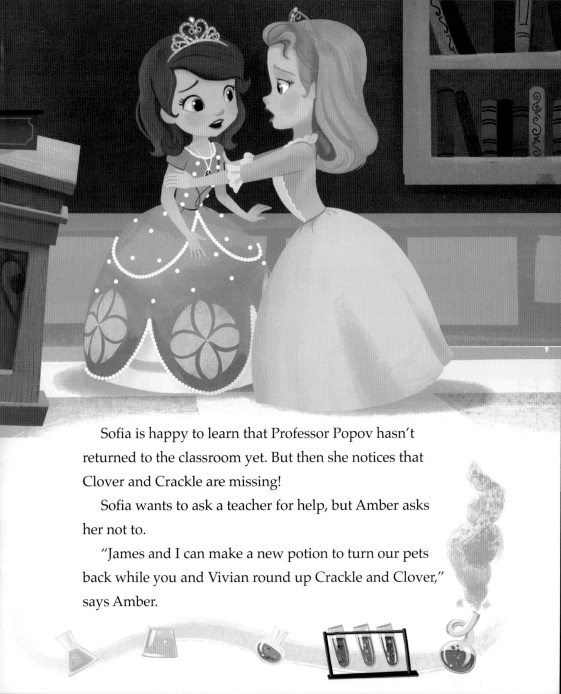

Sofia is happy to learn that Professor Popov hasn't
returned to the classroom yet. But then she notices that
Clover and Crackle are missing!

Sofia wants to ask a teacher for help, but Amber asks
her not to.

"James and I can make a new potion to turn our pets
back while you and Vivian round up Crackle and Clover,"
says Amber.

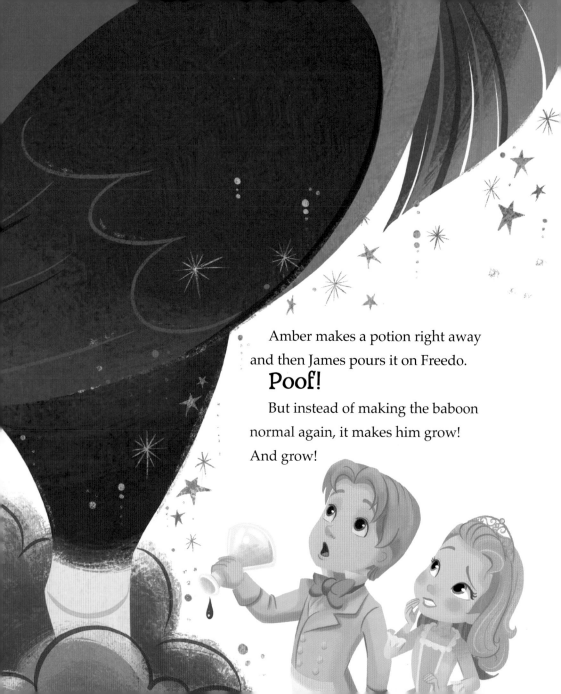

Amber makes a potion right away and then James pours it on Freedo.
Poof!

But instead of making the baboon normal again, it makes him grow! And grow!

Sofia and Vivian soon return to the school with their pets.
Then they hear a loud crash. An enormous Freedo charges
down the hallway, followed by James, Amber and Praline.
"The new potion didn't work," James says.

The kids catch up with Freedo in the school gym. Unfortunately, Flora and Fauna are there with the new royal student!

Sofia steps up to explain everything to the fairies. "We brought our pets to school. We shouldn't have done it," she admits. "And then there was an accident."

"Well, two accidents, really," James adds.

"Children, we have rules for a reason," says Flora.

"To keep all of you safe," says Fauna.

"And to keep giant beasts from wrecking our gymnasium," Flora adds.

Each fairy holds out a bottle of potion: one to shrink Freedo and one to unscramble the pets.

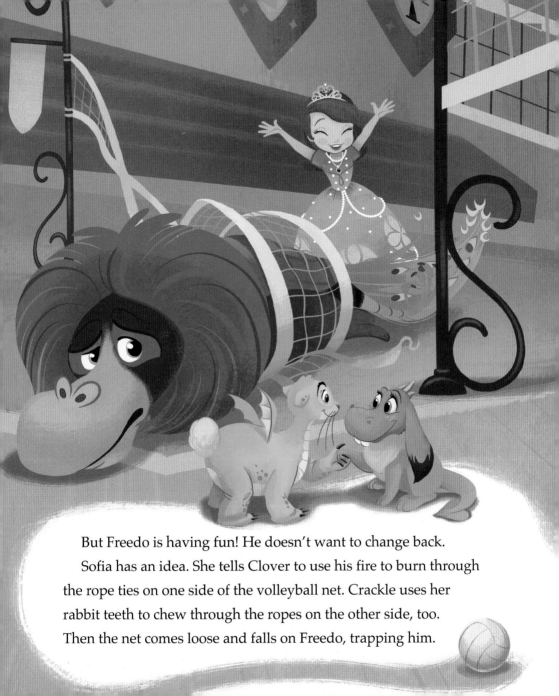

But Freedo is having fun! He doesn't want to change back.

Sofia has an idea. She tells Clover to use his fire to burn through the rope ties on one side of the volleyball net. Crackle uses her rabbit teeth to chew through the ropes on the other side, too. Then the net comes loose and falls on Freedo, trapping him.

The potions are poured on the pets.
Poof!
They're back.

As everyone walks home, Sofia apologizes to Clover.

"I'm just glad I'm back. One hundred per cent pure, 24-carat Clover!" says the bunny.

"Woo-hoo!" Crackle chimes in as she breathes fire happily.